About the Book

A legend is told in Mexico by the people who make sombreros, of two brothers, Andres and Francisco. On their first journey away from home, they were sent to sell the sombreros that their mother had made.

In this book, Mariana Prieto has retold the legend of the white sombreros. It is a tale set against the magnificent color of Mexico, but it is also the appealing story of two brothers and how they faced their first venture. Andres faced his task unafraid, but Francisco lacked his brother's courage.

The boys meet many hazards on their journey: Wasps attack their burros, and playful monkeys almost destroy their sombreros. But it is the determination of Andres that leads the brothers to unexpected rewards and to maturity.

Rober Quackenbush has created light, colorful, and imaginative illustrations in keeping with the legendary aspect and the locale of the story.

To Bill Hill

Copyright © 1969 by HARVEY HOUSE, INC.

All rights reserved, including
the right to reproduce this book
or portions thereof in any form.

Library of Congress Catalog Card No.: 69-10586
Manufactured in the United States of America

HARVEY HOUSE, INC.
Publishers
Irvington-on-Hudson, N.Y. 10533

Mariana Prieto

WHEN THE MONKEYS WORE SOMBREROS

Illustrated by Robert Quackenbush

Once long ago, in the hills of Mexico, lived two brothers. One brother was named Andres. He was short and round like a lima bean. The other brother was named Francisco. He was long and thin like a string bean. They lived in the country where wheat is grown.

Their mother, like all the other women, wove broad-brimmed hats, called *sombreros*. She wove them from *paja trigazo,* or wheat straw. She and their father always took the sombreros to the market to sell. But one day she decided the boys should make the journey.

"You are old enough now to take the sombreros to market,"
she told them. "Your father and I have work to do here."

"Bueno!" Andres said. "I am brave. I know we can make it
all right." His big black eyes were bright and sure.

10

"I do not know, Mama," Francisco said anxiously. "The way is long and many things can happen." He waved his long, thin arms hopelessly.

"Don't be silly," Andres said. "We can get there all right. If we have trouble, I am sure we will find someone to help us."

So they went and got their little burros and piled the sombreros high on the backs of the animals. When they had tied the sombreros in place, they climbed on their burros and started off for the market.

It was a long, hot ride, but Andres sang as he rode. He might not have, had he known what lay ahead for them.

13

When night came, the boys made camp. They tied the burros
to nearby orange trees.

"I saw a wasp fly by," Francisco said. "There must be nests
in those trees. Surely the wasps will sting our burros and something terrible will happen."

"Nonsense," said Andres. "If there are wasps flying around,
they will keep thieves from stealing our sombreros."

The boys untied the mountains of sombreros from the burros and placed them nearby. Then, after feeding their animals, they ate some cold *tortillas*. Finally, they rolled themselves in their ponchos and went to rest on the ground. Soon they were fast asleep.

15

They slept until daybreak. The birds calling and singing woke them up.

"We must get an early start," Andres said.

So they got up and placed the sombreros on the backs of the little burros.

They had just tied the piles of sombreros and returned to roll up their ponchos, when the wasps came.

The wasps attacked the burros. The burros brayed in fury and dashed about. The boys wanted to help, but they were afraid of getting stung, so they stayed at a safe distance.

In their panic, the little burros broke the ropes that tied them to the trees. As the wasps stung them, they were like wild bucking horses, not mild little burros. The cords that held the sombreros in place broke, and the sombreros spilled all over the ground, while the boys rushed about picking them up.

Suddenly overhead in the orange trees a terrible chattering began. The trees were filled with monkeys.

The monkeys, seeing the sombreros on the ground, scurried down the trees and began gathering them up. They put the sombreros on their heads, laughing and chattering to one another.

"Now we're in real trouble," Francisco said. "What are we to do?"

21

The little burros, in the meantime, had galloped down to a nearby stream. They rolled in the water and drowned the wasps. But Andres and Francisco did not solve their problem so easily.

The boys picked up some pebbles and threw them at the monkeys. The monkeys in turn picked oranges from the trees and threw them at the boys. But they went on grabbing sombreros.

The oranges plopped to the ground. They broke open and splattered the sombreros that lay there. The boys, too, were splattered with juice from the same oranges.

"We are in a hopeless state," Francisco said "Let's go home."

"No, no," said Andres, as he kept on throwing pebbles.

At that moment, an old man came along. He stared in surprise at the strange scene.

The monkeys swung from tree to tree, wearing the sombreros
and tossing them back and forth to each other.

"Chee, chee," Andres screamed at the monkeys. "Vaya, go

"Keep on throwing pebbles," he ordered Francisco.

At last the monkeys did seem to tire of their game. Some of them took off the sombreros and tossed them to the ground. But others went leaping away into the dense, green thicket, still wearing the hats. When they were gone, the boys began picking up the sombreros, which were all spotted and sticky with orange juice.

"I told you it was hopeless," Francisco said.

"You give up too easily," said Andres. "Let's take these sombreros down to the stream and wash them."

26

The old man watched as the boys gathered up the sombreros,

and shook his head. He followed the boys to the stream.

27

The boys found their burros by the stream. When they saw that the burros were all right, they tied them to trees and gave them some sugar. Then they began to wash the soiled sombreros. They washed and washed, but they could not get the sombreros clean.

"What shall we do?" Francisco asked, half in tears. "Our sombreros are ruined, and Mother and Father will be very angry. I knew something terrible like this would happen."

"Quiet," Andres said. "There must be some way to clean these sombreros. We were told to sell them in the market, so sell them we will."

The old man, who had been sitting silently nearby, spoke at last.

"You boys have had a terrible time and I want to help you. I have some bleach that I made from ground clam shells. Perhaps this will remove the orange-juice stains. Come, bring the sombreros to my house and we will try."

29

So the boys took the wet sombreros to the old man's house. They used the bleach on the sombreros and spread them to dry in the sun.

The sun was high now and it was very hot. The sombreros dried quickly. They dried a gleaming white, and the stains were gone.

"Oh, no," said Francisco. "Look at our sombreros now! They don't look like the sombreros that other people make. Surely, no one will want them."

"We will try to sell them anyway," said Andres. "Come, help me load them on the burros."

So they walked back to the stream with the sombreros and fastened them to the backs of their burros. Then they thanked the old man and went on their way.

At the market, people gathered around the boys when they
unloaded their sombreros. No one had seen such white sombreros
before. The people liked them and they all wanted to buy them.
Almost at once, the boys had sold all of their sombreros.

When the boys were home again, they told their mother and father what had happened to them. Andres told the secret of how they had bleached the sombreros. And Francisco told how quickly they had sold them.

Their parents decided from that day on to bleach all of their sombreros. They sold them as fast as they could make them, and they all became very rich.

One afternoon, while they were working, Francisco said to Andres: "You had the courage to keep on trying. That is why our trip was a success. In spite of all that happened, we came out well in the end because of your bravery. I should have been the brave one, because I am older. But from now on, little brother, I am going to be as brave as you are."

He smiled, and picked up one of the sombreros and put it jauntily on his head.

And they both laughed.

And so ends the legend that is told by the people in Mexico who make sombreros.

About the Author

MARIANA PRIETO, born in Cincinnati, Ohio, and educated in Cuba, is a bilingual writer in Spanish and English. Her multi-ethnic and interracial stories for boys and girls appeal equally to children of both nationalities. One of her books, *A Kite for Carlos*, was recommended by The National Council of Christians and Jews, Books for Brotherhood.

Miss Prieto has traveled and studied in Mexico, Yucatan, The Bahamas, Jamaica, and Puerto Rico. Currently she is teaching classes in creative writing in Miami, Florida.

About the Illustrator

ROBERT QUACKENBUSH has illustrated over twenty-five children's books and classics. He is also the recipient of numerous prizes and awards. Two recent books illustrated by him are Junior Literary Guild selections. His graphics have been exhibited in museums throughout the United States including the Whitney Museum and the Philadelphia Academy of Fine Arts. Born in Arizona and educated in California, Mr. Quackenbush now resides in New York.